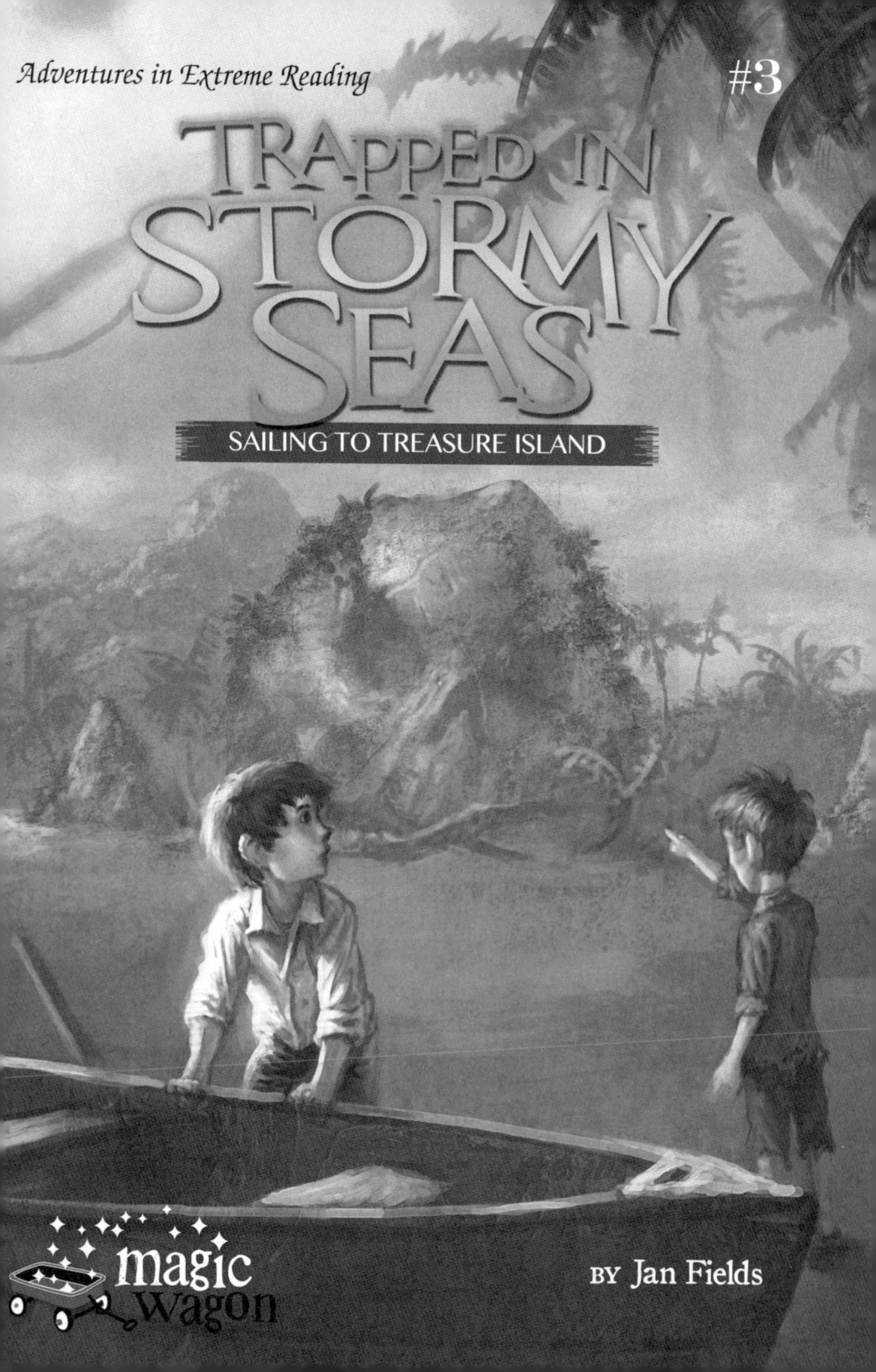

Adventures in Extreme Reading

#3

TRAPPED IN STORMY SEAS

SAILING TO TREASURE ISLAND

magic Wagon

BY Jan Fields

visit us at www.abdopublishing.com

Calico Chapter Books™ is a trademark and logo of Magic Wagon.

Printed in the United States of America, North Mankato, Minnesota.
102012
012013
This book contains at least 10% recycled materials.

Written by Jan Fields
Cover illustration by Scott Altmann
Edited by Stephanie Hedlund and Grace Hansen
Cover and interior design by Neil Klinepier

Library of Congress Cataloging-in-Publication Data

Fields, Jan.
  Trapped in stormy seas : sailing to Treasure Island / by Jan Fields ;
[illustrator, Scott Altmann].
     p. cm. -- (Adventures in extreme reading ; bk. 3)
  Summary: Their Uncle Dan is still missing and Carter and Isabelle
are starting to worry, especially after they receive a threatening call
from the computer hacker--and he challenges them to match wits
with him in Treasure Island.
  ISBN 978-1-61641-921-9
1. Stevenson, Robert Louis, 1850-1894. Treasure Island--Juvenile
fiction. 2. Virtual reality--Juvenile fiction. 3. Computer hackers--
Juvenile fiction. 4. Books and reading--Juvenile fiction. 5. Inventions-
-Juvenile fiction. 6. Cousins--Juvenile fiction. [1. Stevenson, Robert
Louis, 1850-1894. Treasure Island--Fiction. 2. Virtual reality--Fiction.
3. Computer hackers--Fiction. 4. Books and reading--Fiction. 5.
Inventions--Fiction. 6. Cousins--Fiction.] I. Altmann, Scott, ill. II.
Title.
  PZ7.F479177Tr 2013
  813.6--dc23
                                        2012028639

Table of Contents

WHERE'S UNCLE DAN?

Carter Lewis tilted the game remote to the left to send his cow galloping through a row of scarecrows. He mowed them down then twisted the remote backward so the cow sailed over the fence.

His buddy Matt's cow took another wild run off the road, since Matt was laughing so hard he couldn't steer. Cow racing was the goofiest video game either guy could imagine, but they loved it.

Carter's cow galloped over the finish line well ahead of Matt's. Carter gave his friend a cheerful whack on the back.

"I win," he said. "Again."

"I can't help it," Matt said, flopping backward onto the couch. "Those cows crack me up."

Just then, the ominous tones of Darth Vader's March rang out from Carter's hoodie pocket. He rolled his eyes. "My cousin is calling."

Grinning, Matt began the deep, gasping sounds of Darth Vader as Carter put the phone to his ear. "What do you want, Izzy?"

"Meet me at Uncle Dan's. Now."

"I'm a little busy."

Izzy hung up. Carter growled and threw his phone down on the couch. It bounced once and ended up in Matt's lap.

"You know," Matt said as he handed back the phone, "you really shouldn't let Isabelle get to you like that. Besides, she's not that bad."

"Not that bad? Compared to what?"

Matt shrugged. "Some guys might even think she's kind of cute," he mumbled.

"Crazy guys." Carter sighed. "I guess I better go. It might be something important. I'll talk to you later."

The bike ride to Uncle Dan's was a little farther from Matt's house than from Carter's. It gave him a chance to think about what Isabelle might be worked up about. The last message from their uncle had said he was closing in on the hacker who was after his invention.

Uncle Dan had created the coolest possible way to "read" a book. Instead of looking at words on a page, Uncle Dan's invention let you actually go inside the world of the story and live it. He'd made virtual reality suits that let you see, smell, hear, and feel the book. Sometimes the result was scary, but it was always cool.

Unfortunately, a hacker called Storm had gotten in Uncle Dan's system. Storm added scary stuff to all of the books. Carter had almost been stabbed by a musketeer and bitten by a rabbit with steel teeth.

Maybe Uncle Dan had brought Storm back to his house. Maybe he had the creep tied up in the basement and wanted Izzy and Carter to help him get the guy to talk.

"Not very likely," Carter muttered as he pedaled faster. "Still, you never know."

Finally he raced onto Uncle Dan's driveway and hopped off his bike. He stowed it behind the trash corral next to Izzy's. His uncle was a little paranoid about people knowing his business. He always had Izzy and Carter hide their bikes from spying eyes.

Carter didn't even bother checking for the spare key. Izzy never put it back if she made it inside first. He huffed with annoyance and rang the bell. The door flew open and a skinny arm reached out. It grabbed the front of his hoodie and jerked him inside. Carter yelped. He stumbled a little when his cousin let him go so she could slam the door behind him.

"What's with you?" he demanded. "Is Uncle Dan back?"

Izzy turned and shook her head. Carter noticed she was even paler than usual and her eyes were red. Had she been crying? He took a step back. He totally didn't know what to do with a crying girl.

"Uncle Dan is missing," Isabelle whispered.

"Missing? He's probably just off questioning Storm. You know he doesn't check in much."

"He's missing," she repeated, following him as he headed upstairs toward the fridge. "I checked Uncle Dan's e-mail. All of his contacts are looking for him. That means they don't know where he is. So he's missing."

"Or busy," Carter insisted. He rooted in the fridge for a can of soda, then settled gloomily for a juice box. "He might be roughing Storm up, and he doesn't want any witnesses."

"You think Uncle Dan would hurt someone?"

Carter paused. His uncle was really more of a brains over brawn guy. In fact, he was tall but scrawny like Carter. "Maybe," he mumbled.

"Sure, and he might secretly be a ninja," Izzy said. "But he's not."

"You still don't know that he's missing," Carter insisted stubbornly. "Uncle Dan has always been a little strange. Maybe he just doesn't want to be found."

Izzy shook her head, her long, blonde hair

falling like a curtain over her face. "There's something wrong. I can feel it."

Carter shrugged. Izzy was starting to make him nervous. What if something was wrong? "We could try calling him," he suggested.

Isabelle opened her eyes wide. "On what? He thinks cell phones are a government plot to spy on people."

"He does. Still, he took one with him." Carter folded his arms over his chest, happy to be the one with secret information. "It was one of those disposables. Just in case."

Izzy socked him in the arm. "Why didn't you tell me that? I've been scared to death."

Carter fought the urge to rub his sore arm. "It was a secret. He gave me the number. He told me to memorize it and eat the paper or something. I'm not that good at the whole memorizing thing. I wrote it inside my shoe. Hold on." He sat on the edge of one of his uncle's kitchen stools and pulled off his shoe. "See?"

Isabelle grabbed the shoe and peered inside. She wrinkled her nose, but she didn't make a single rude comment about the smell. Carter realized she must really be worried if she passed up a cheap shot about his stinky feet.

"It's a little faded," she said as she dug her cell phone out of her pocket. "But I can read it."

She punched buttons, then she tossed the shoe back into Carter's lap. He watched her pull on her lower lip with her teeth as she waited for their uncle to answer. Finally, the call must have rolled over to voice mail. She sighed and said, "Uncle Dan, no one seems to know where you are. We're worried. Can you call or e-mail or something?"

Izzy stuffed the phone back in her pocket and walked to the fridge. Carter heard her sniff as she rooted around, pretending to look for a soda.

"Try not to worry," he said. He felt a little panicky when he realized she might be crying again. "He'll probably call you really soon."

She nodded but didn't turn around for another minute or two. Carter wondered if you could get frostbite on your face from staring into the fridge like that. Then she swiped at her eyes with one hand and grabbed a juice box with the other. He was glad to see she wasn't crying when she looked at him, but her eyes did look redder.

"You're probably right," she said, her voice sounding funny. "He's going to call soon."

As if in answer, they heard the antique telephone ringtone that Izzy used for her cell phone. She almost dropped her juice box as she hurried to pull out her phone.

"It's Uncle Dan's number," she yelped. "Uncle Dan?"

Suddenly her face grew pale. She pulled the phone away from her ear as if it had stung her. She quickly hit the speakerphone button.

"We've only met virtually so far," a robotic-sounding voice said, "but now we're going to get to know each other much better. As you can hear, I have your uncle's phone. I also have your uncle. If you want to see him alive again, you'll do exactly as I say."

"What do you want?" Izzy asked.

"I want you to reformat your uncle's computers," the voice said. "Then remove his hard drives and burn them. Then we'll talk about what to do with those virtual suits."

"You want us to destroy Uncle Dan's work?" Carter yelped.

"Either that," the voice said, "or I destroy your uncle. Your choice. But choose quickly. When the storm hits, someone dies."

Carter looked into his cousin's wide eyes. What were they going to do?

STORM FRONT

"**W**hy do you want us to destroy Uncle Dan's computer?" Izzy shouted, smacking her hand on the counter so hard it made the phone jump. "What's it to you, anyway?"

"That is not your concern," the robotic voice responded. The flat, even tone contrasted sharply with Isabelle's near hysteria. "Your uncle should be your concern."

"Why not tell us?" Carter asked. He thought maybe Izzy was stalling for time while she came up with some kind of brilliant computer geek answer to all this. At least, he hoped she was.

"You're not scared two kids could do anything about it, are you?" Carter taunted.

"Ha, ha," the voice said flatly. "You're still

not focused on what's important, kiddies."

"You're scared," Carter said. "Since I figured out your name, you're scared we might beat you again."

"You're fooling yourself, kid."

A vague idea raced around Carter's head and he grabbed at it. "If you're not scared, what about another contest? You like games. I know you do. How about we compete inside one of Uncle Dan's books. Assuming you can hack your way back inside again."

"Why would I play this game?" the voice asked. "I already have your uncle."

"Right!" Izzy shouted. "You're just a common kidnapper. Why risk losing now when you hold the cards? Especially since Carter beat you once."

"That was a fluke," the robotic voice stayed completely flat, but Carter and Izzy could still tell they were getting under the hacker's skin. "I went easy on you because you're children."

"So don't go easy on us this time," Carter

said. "Let us prove we can play and win. One contest and if we win, you release Uncle Dan. If you win, we destroy the computers and suits."

"You'll destroy the suits and computers now. You'll do it or your uncle will pay the price."

"Just like you said," Izzy said, dropping her voice to a stage whisper as she pretended to talk to Carter. "Chicken."

"I am not fooled by this ploy. You will follow my directions or I will kill your uncle. No playing needed."

"I'm not destroying anything until I'm sure Uncle Dan is okay," Isabelle said, changing tactics. "How do I know you haven't already killed him? How do I know you have him at all? You could have just picked his pocket and taken the phone. Put him on the phone or forget it."

With that, the call ended. Carter and Isabelle both stared at the phone.

"What do you think that means?" Carter asked. "Do you think the call dropped? Or did we make him so mad he hung up on us?"

Isabelle glared at him. "Do you see a crystal ball in front of me? I don't know."

"Maybe we should call the police," Carter said.

Isabelle sat on one of the stools beside Carter. She squinted in thought for a moment, then said, "I'm not sure we should. If Storm calls back and lets us talk with Uncle Dan, he might feed us some clues. Uncle Dan is good at that kind of thing."

Carter nodded. He and Uncle Dan had all kinds of secret codes. Some were just for fun and some were because Uncle Dan was the most paranoid person Carter had ever met. How could Storm have grabbed him? Uncle Dan was so careful about security.

"But what if Storm doesn't call back?"

Isabelle looked thoughtful for a moment. "We'll wait an hour. If he hasn't called back, we can call the police."

"Okay. In that case, I'm going to find

something to eat." Carter hopped off the stool and began to rummage around in Uncle Dan's cupboards.

"How can you eat at a time like this?" Izzy asked in disbelief.

"I'm starving," he said. "Where are all the cereal bars and fruit leather?"

"I ate them," she said. "I've been spending hours here working on the coding for those books. I had to eat something."

Carter turned to the fridge. All he found inside was a jar of sweet pickles and an old carton of vanilla yogurt. He tossed the carton in the trash and settled down at the counter with the pickle jar. He offered one to his cousin but she just shook her head.

For a little while, the only sound was the crunch of pickles. Suddenly, the phone rang. Isabelle pounced on it.

"Your uncle does not feel up to chatting right now," Storm said.

"What have you done to him?" Izzy shrieked.

"If you've hurt him—" Carter growled.

"If I've hurt him, he'll heal. I've been thinking about your other offer. I'm not fooled by this ploy," Storm said, "but I do find games entertaining, and your uncle isn't going anywhere. Plus, you cannot possibly win. So, fine. I'll play. I'll contact you with the rules of the game." The phone went dead.

"I don't like it that we didn't get to talk to Uncle Dan," Carter said. "He could be hurt, or worse."

"I don't like it either, but at least Storm is willing to play the game."

"Did we just do something really smart or really stupid?" Carter asked.

"Smart," Izzy said. "Let's get down to Uncle Dan's office before Storm calls back. It's possible I can find a way to trace the call, then we could send someone to rescue Uncle Dan."

The two raced down the stairs and Isabelle said the password to let them into Uncle Dan's basement office filled with computers. The perfectly neat tabletops proved Izzy had been the only one working down here. Uncle Dan felt messiness was a sign of creativity, while Isabelle was the ultimate neat freak.

"You know, when Uncle Dan does get home," Carter said, "you're going to be in so much trouble for all this neatness."

"Right now, getting yelled at by Uncle Dan sounds pretty good," Izzy said as she settled into the chair in front of the main computer and began typing. Carter glanced over her shoulder, but the commands she typed didn't mean much to him. He loved to play games, but he didn't really share the computer nerd skills of Uncle Dan and Izzy.

"So how can you trace the call?" Carter asked. "We already know it came from Uncle Dan's phone."

"Most new cell phones have GPS," Izzy said as she typed. "So unless he's disabled that, I should be able to track the phone that way."

"The cell phone company lets you do that?"

Carter asked.

Izzy shook her head. "Not exactly. It's a little bit illegal."

Carter wondered if it made him a good citizen or a bad nephew that he didn't like this idea. "Maybe we should call the police and let them use the cell phone to find him."

Izzy didn't answer for a minute or two as she leaned close to the flashing text on the screen. Finally, she slumped back in the chair with a groan. "The GPS has been disabled. Unless Storm makes a 911 call with Uncle Dan's phone, the GPS won't reset."

Carter let out the breath he had not realized he was holding. "So what do we do now?"

Isabelle's shoulders slumped. "We wait for Storm to call back."

"I still think we should think about calling the police," Carter said. "They're professionals at this kind of thing."

"Who knows more about Storm, the police or us?" Izzy asked. "And if I can't track the cell phone, neither can they."

Carter frowned. He wasn't sure if he believed Izzy really knew more than the police. Didn't they handle kidnappings all the time? On television, the police swooped in, pulled clues out of nowhere, and then rushed off to save the day. He scuffed his foot on the floor while he tried to decide if he should argue with his cousin about this.

The ringing of Izzy's phone made them both jump. Izzy lunged for the phone where she'd set it on Uncle Dan's desk, but her hands were shaking so hard she nearly sent it skittering to the floor. Carter caught it just in time and handed it to her.

"Hello," she said, her voice trembling.

The mechanical voice of Storm came through the phone's speakers again. "I've decided to play the game with you. Here's my challenge. I pick the book. I've hacked your uncle's system already, so I will enter the book by becoming one of the characters. Your challenge is to guess which one is me. But my character may not be the only change I make."

"How many guesses do I get?" Carter asked.

"One," Storm said.

Izzy licked her lips and glanced nervously at Carter. She raised her eyebrows in question and he nodded. "Okay, we can accept that. All we have to do is figure out which character is really being played by you."

"Right," Storm said. "Now what challenge do you set for me?"

"I need to know what book you want so I can decide," Izzy said.

"I pick *Treasure Island.*"

Isabelle snorted. "Sure, a book full of killers and thieves."

Carter almost whooped. He'd actually read that one. Actually he hadn't read it himself, but it was a book his dad had read aloud to him when he was younger. He knew that book! He grinned and nodded at Izzy.

She looked thoughtful for a moment. "Okay,

that book will be acceptable. For our challenge, I'll move the treasure. To win, you have to find it."

The phone was silent for a moment. Then the flat voice said, "You'll have to give clues."

"I'll give one," Izzy responded.

"Four," Storm said.

"In that case, we get four guesses for which character has been replaced by you," Izzy said.

"Two," the voice answered. "Don't forget who holds the trump card."

"We aren't likely to forget that," Carter said. "How do I make my guesses in this game?"

"Just confront the character with your guess."

"Okay. That deal sounds fine," Izzy said.

"When do we suit up?" Carter asked. Then a sudden thought hit him. "How do you suit up? You're not coming here to use one of Uncle Dan's suits?" The thought of facing Storm in person made his heart pound. Still, if the hacker came to Uncle Dan's house, they could call the police and let them handle this.

"I have a suit of my own," Storm said. "I doubt it is exactly like the ones your uncle created, but it should be compatible with his system. We will suit up tomorrow morning at six AM. We can chat after I win."

"Or we win," Izzy snapped, but she was talking to a dial tone. Storm had hung up.

"Can you come up with a good hiding place for the treasure?" Carter asked.

"I guess I'll have to, won't I?" Then she paused. "The thing is, I've never read *Treasure Island.*"

"Oh yeah, that's right." Carter still couldn't believe he'd actually sort of read a classic that Izzy hadn't. "That's okay though. I have."

"So you know where the treasure is?"

Carter nodded.

"Then I guess Uncle Dan's life is in your hands."

To that, Carter had nothing to say at all.

A PIRATE'S LIFE FOR ME

It turned out that Carter's memory wasn't quite as specific as it needed to be. Carter knew that the treasure in the book wasn't where the treasure map said. And that it had been moved by another pirate. But he couldn't remember exactly where it ended up.

"I remember there was a fort on the island," he told Izzy. "But I think the treasure was in a cave or a volcano or something."

"The island had a volcano?" Izzy asked.

Carter shifted nervously. "Maybe."

Ultimately, they had to spend some time skimming the book. They found the full text online. "I didn't know you could just find whole books like that online," he said.

Izzy didn't answer as she carefully used the

computer mouse to draw a map of the island. Every line that described the actual land, Izzy added the detail to the map. Carter found the whole process painfully boring.

He tried to stay focused. Uncle Dan was depending on him. But when Izzy erased a small cove on her map for the third time, he groaned. They'd been sitting in the basement for hours, and he was starving.

Izzy looked sideways at him. "You don't have to stay."

"I need to stay and help."

"Sighing and groaning isn't helping. It's just bugging me."

"Are you sure?" Carter said, squirming to keep from running for the door too fast.

"I'm sure. Besides, you need to go read the book again. Or at least skim it. Pay attention to the characters. You need to be able to pick out the one that doesn't belong."

Carter groaned inside. Now Izzy was giving him homework. But he had sense enough to keep quiet and nod. Then he bolted.

As he rode his bike home, thoughts of Uncle Dan made his empty stomach knot. He hoped he was doing the right thing by going along with Isabelle on this. Plus, he wasn't sure he could even hold up his end. He liked *Treasure Island*, but it had been a couple years since his dad had read it to him.

When Carter got to his house, he snagged a microwave burrito and headed into the office. His dad was doing the monthly bill paying, which normally included a lot of scowling and muttering. Carter stepped in the door and peered across the room at the bookshelves.

"Can I help you?" his dad asked just after Carter had shoved a quarter of the burrito into his mouth.

"I'b ookig o' boo."

His dad held up his hand. "I don't need a burrito shower. Chew, swallow, and tell me what you need."

Carter chewed a little and then swallowed

the huge lump. "I'm looking for *Treasure Island*. I want to read it."

His dad looked surprised, then suspicious. "Why?"

Carter paused. For an instant, he considered pouring out the whole story. Then his shoulders sagged. His dad would call the police. Any sensible person would call the police. If something horrible happened to Uncle Dan, would it be Carter's fault for not telling?

Finally he sighed. "I want to read it. I really enjoyed it when you read it to me before." That much was true, at least.

"Is it homework?"

"No, I just want to read it."

Carter felt a pang of guilt as his dad's face lit up when he pointed across the room. "That's great. It's on the right, near the bottom. Try not to get burrito stains on it, okay?"

Carter stuffed the last of the burrito in his mouth and wiped his hands on his jeans. Then he grabbed the book. His dad waved him off.

"Enjoy it. When you're done, I've got some other great books."

Great, Carter thought. *Do one brainy thing and your parents expect it to be a new lifestyle.* He stalked out of the room and headed off to read.

As he skimmed the book, he saw that some characters could be marked off right away. Storm wouldn't choose to be a character who died early in the book or one who only appeared in a single chapter. The hacker would need to choose a character who made it all the way to the island so he could search for the treasure.

Carter knew who he would pick if he were Storm. He'd be Long John Silver. Silver controlled almost everything. Plus, if Storm liked pirates, Long John Silver had to be nearly irresistible. He decided to keep special watch on the pirate.

Carter was still reading when he finally nodded off to sleep. His dreams were full of swords, muskets, and searching for treasure.

INTO THE BOOK

The next day, Carter made sure to eat a huge breakfast before heading over to Uncle Dan's house. He knew he might be spending most of the day in the suit. Then all the food he'd have the chance to eat would be virtual. The suit could offer small sips of water, if he had his character drink something. Uncle Dan hadn't figured out a way to feed you. A guy could starve on virtual food.

Carter wasn't surprised to find Isabelle at the house when he got there. She looked worn out. Her long, straight blonde hair was pulled back with a rubber band from Uncle Dan's desk. The skin under her eyes looked purple.

"Did you go home at all last night?" Carter asked.

Isabelle shook her head as her fingers flew over the keyboard. She stopped and looked at him.

"I told my folks I was sleeping over at a friend's house," she said. "They were excited. Sleepovers are so girly."

Carter had to admit that *girly* wasn't a word he normally thought of when describing Isabelle. Now *nerdy* popped into his head quite often, along with *bossy*. Isabelle's hoarse voice pulled his attention back on her.

"I've created a character for you to play," she said. "That way you can logically be in every scene. You're Jim's cousin and best friend. You're an orphan who lives at his parents' inn."

Carter nodded, remembering that the book began at the inn. "Have you moved the treasure?" he asked.

"I've removed it from the cave," she said. "But I haven't relocated it yet. So maybe you could go get a soda or do your pacing upstairs while I finish."

Carter froze. He hadn't been pacing exactly. More like shifting back and forth. Still, he guessed that could be pretty distracting.

"Where are you going to put it?" he asked.

Isabelle had already turned back to the keyboard. Her fingers flew over the keys again. She didn't speak. Carter huffed in annoyance but turned toward the door. As long as she told him before they suited up, he could wait.

Carter's hand was on the door leading to the stairs when the phone beside Isabelle rang. She gave a small shriek and grabbed for it. Carter was too far away to catch it before it hit the floor. Isabelle had to scramble for it.

"Hello," she said.

"I am ready," the mechanical voice of Storm said. "Which of you will be entering the suit?"

"Carter," Isabelle said.

"Good. Have him do so now."

"I'm not done with my coding," Izzy said.

"Finish it after we've entered the game,"

Storm responded. "The time for waiting is over. I expect a quick resolution to this challenge. And then you will connect a Webcam so I can watch you destroy the suits and the computers."

"Not if we win," Carter snapped.

"I like that spirit. It will make beating you all the more satisfying. Enter the book. I will be waiting."

Carter stomped over and jerked open the door of the suit room. The two virtual reality suits hung from the ceiling by cables and wires. They looked like some kind of huge astronaut puppets. He heard Isabelle follow him inside, but he never paused. He simply pulled open the back of one suit and stepped in.

For a moment, light seeped through the opening in the back of the suit. When Isabelle closed the back seam, the suit seemed to tighten around Carter. He was surrounded by total darkness. Carter felt a small thrill of fear.

Total darkness was something Carter rarely experienced. At home, street lights shone through the window at night. Even the basement in his house had multiple windows where dusty light seeped in even before you flipped the switch. The darkness of the closed suit was absolute.

As the suit molded automatically to his body in order to give him the most lifelike experience, Carter felt like a rabbit caught in the coils of a snake. He breathed hard as he fought panic. What was taking Izzy so long?

Light exploded against his eyes and he blinked.

"Cousin!"

Carter turned sharply at the voice and found himself looking at a boy about the same age as him with a thick head of dark blond hair. "Come on," the boy said, pulling on Carter's sleeve. "There's a real pirate in the inn or my name isn't Jim Hawkins. Father is speaking with him now."

Carter followed, almost tripping on the strange, ill-fitting shoes he wore. The soles of the shoes felt smooth, making every step a little slippery. He also had some kind of odd short pants, tall socks, and a slightly rough white shirt. In fact, none of the fabric was exactly smooth. Carter suspected he was going to spend a lot of this adventure scratching.

The boys came around the corner to see a tall, rugged-looking man. Every part of him looked dirty and ragged, from his dirt-caked fingernails to his mended blue coat. He had a long, black ponytail that hung limp with grease. Across one cheek, a white scar stood out like lightning against his sun-darkened skin. All he needed was a peg leg, a hook hand, and an eye patch to make a perfect movie pirate.

The man was drinking some golden liquid from a thick glass. He sipped it almost daintily, then smacked his lips. "Much company, mate?" he asked the thin, pale man behind the bar.

"That would be good for business," the thin man said. "But sadly, no."

The shabby pirate smiled a bit then. "Well,

then," he said, "this is the berth for me." He looked around sharply and caught sight of Carter and Jim peering around the corner. "Here, boys. I've left my chest outside. Fetch it in for me. I'll stay here a bit."

Jim looked at the thin man behind the counter. The man nodded and Carter realized he was Jim's father. Jim caught Carter's arm again and pulled him along to the door. Behind them, Carter heard the old pirate speaking. "You can call me *Captain*."

Jim hurried toward the door and Carter followed him as the old pirate described the sort of food and drink he liked to Jim's father. Outside, the boys found the seaman's chest in a wheelbarrow. Beside it, a bony young man sat on the inn steps and cleaned his nails with the tip of a knife. Carter was pretty sure this part wasn't in the book. Did that mean Storm was already here? He looked sharply between Jim and the ragged young man.

"The captain will be lodging here," Jim told

the man. "We're taking his chest up to his room."

The young man frowned. "I was hoping for some coin."

"The captain didn't pay you?" Jim asked.

"He did," the young man said. "But it's always nice to see a little extra jingle."

"Well, I've none for you."

For a moment, Carter thought the other boy might fight them over it. The boy looked up at Carter, who knew he looked even taller on the high step where he stood. The boy seemed to decide a fight wasn't such a good idea after all. Instead, he stomped off after dumping the sea chest out of his wheelbarrow and into the dirt. Carter made a mental note to keep an eye out for that character. If he returned, he might be Storm.

Jim grabbed one handle at the end of the chest and cleared his throat as Carter continued to stare at it. Carter finally took the hint and grabbed his end. They hauled the chest up the stairs. It was about the size of a college foot locker, but made of leather and iron. The corners were somewhat smashed and broken. In the center of the lid, someone had burned a rough letter B.

"You see what I mean," Jim said in a rough whisper as they trudged up the narrow wooden stairs. "A pirate captain right here at the Admiral Benbow Inn."

"I don't think he's a captain," Carter said. "He just likes to think of himself that way."

"What makes you think that?" Jim asked.

"Just a feeling I have," Carter said.

Suddenly, he heard Isabelle's voice saying his name in his ear. It startled him so much, he dropped his end of the chest with a thump. He twisted around on the stairs, expecting to see her behind him.

"Are you daft?" Jim snapped. "If you break this open, Father will be furious. And I expect that pirate captain isn't one to spare the rod either."

"Sorry," Carter muttered, picking up his end

of the chest. He lowered his voice to a whisper. "What do you want, Izzy?"

Jim shot him an odd look but didn't comment.

"I just wanted to tell you that I'm going to jump the book ahead a little. There's no point in spending much time at the inn with characters who disappear from the book. None of these characters could be Storm, except maybe Jim. Anyway, things are going to go a little wonky for a second."

"Okay, but let me put down this chest first," Carter whispered fiercely. "And let me get off these stairs."

"Who are you talking to?" Jim asked.

They'd reached the top of the stairs so Carter just shrugged. "Myself?"

Jim shook his head, then led the way into a small, neat room. They laid the chest on the floor and Carter whispered, "Okay, I'm ready." He hoped he really was.

PiRATES!

The room spun around Carter like a carnival ride and he staggered a little with dizziness. Finally the swirling room settled down. Carter found himself standing in a sweltering hot kitchen. An older woman with worried eyes handed him a mug of something and said, "Carry that in to the doctor."

Carter nodded. He looked around quickly. The room had two doors. Which one would take him to the doctor? The woman sighed and gave Carter a push toward the closer door.

In the hall, Carter spotted Jim following a neatly dressed man wearing a snow-white powdered wig like George Washington always wore in pictures Carter had seen. He realized that must be the doctor and followed them into the parlor.

40

The room had a number of small tables and a half dozen men or so. Carter quickly spotted the old pirate. He was sitting alone at one of the tables in the far corner and muttering. The doctor seemed to spot someone he knew at another table.

"Taylor," the doctor said cheerfully as he settled across from an elderly man, "how are you feeling?"

The old man smiled, showing off empty gums. He said he was well, though bothered some by the rheumatics. Carter had no idea what that was, but he was happy to set the mug down before the doctor and back away.

The old pirate sat up in his chair and launched into song. "Fifteen men on the dead man's chest!"

The doctor glared at the pirate's loud voice, but went on to describe some sort of treatment for the old man. Carter winced when the doctor mentioned putting leeches on the sore spots. He backed farther away so he didn't have to hear any more medical advice. Finally, he reached a wall where he could lean and watch the whole room.

Carter watched Dr. Livesey thoughtfully. The doctor was a character throughout the entire book. He might easily be Storm. Of course, so could Jim Hawkins. Carter looked over at the other boy, but he couldn't see anything suspicious about him.

Suddenly the old pirate slammed his hand upon the table. Everyone but the doctor jumped and fell silent. Carter saw the old man across from the doctor shift nervously, but the doctor seemed totally calm and continued talking.

"Silence, there, between decks!" the pirate growled.

"Were you addressing me, sir?" the doctor asked.

"You know I was," the pirate said.

"I have only one thing to say to you, sir," the doctor replied. "If you keep on the way you are going, the world will soon be free of a very dirty scoundrel!"

The pirate jumped to his feet and pulled a knife from his pocket. "I'll pin you to the wall!"

The doctor didn't even flinch. "If you do not put that knife away this instant, I promise, on my honor, that you will hang."

The doctor and the pirate locked gazes. The pirate turned away first and slipped his knife back in his pocket, grumbling.

"Know that I am watching you, sir," the doctor said. "I will have you hunted down if I hear of any trouble from you."

The pirate didn't make another sound or grumble. The doctor turned back to the elderly man and patted his arm.

Carter crossed his arms and watched the doctor. He certainly acted like Storm, or like Carter could imagine Storm acting. Storm wouldn't be the least afraid of a pretend pirate.

"Izzy?" Carter said. "I think the doctor might be Storm. What do you think?"

"I don't know," she said. "But don't accuse

him until you're sure. We only get two guesses."

Carter nodded.

"We're going to jump ahead again," she warned him.

Carter groaned as the room spun again. He was reminded of Uncle Dan's admission that some people threw up in the suits. If they did a lot of this time hopping, he suspected he was going to find out exactly what that was like.

When the room settled, Carter was still in the parlor. Only now, the room was empty and had a distinct chill, even with the roaring fire.

"Carter," Jim snapped, "come over here and help me lay the breakfast table. The captain will be back any minute and you know he doesn't like to wait."

Carter was halfway to his storybook cousin's side when the parlor door opened. He turned and saw a pale man with a fierce squint. Jim pushed silverware and cloth at Carter. Then he hurried over to the stranger and asked what he could do for the man.

The man sat at one of the tables and looked over to where Carter was trying to figure out the right way to put the silverware and napkin at the captain's table.

"Is that table for my mate Bill?" the pale man asked. When he pointed toward the table with his left hand, Carter saw he was missing two fingers on that hand.

"There is no one here named Bill," Jim said from the doorway. "That table is for the captain. He is staying here."

The thin man chuckled a little. The sound wasn't pleasant. "Has he a cut on one cheek? And is it on the right cheek? My mate Bill has such. So, is my mate Bill in this house?"

"Not now," Carter said.

"He's out walking," Jim added.

"Which way, sonny? Which way is he gone?" the man asked eagerly.

Jim explained where the captain normally took his walks. He added that they expected him soon. Carter watched the thin man and was glad that man's attention was on Jim and not himself.

"I can run ahead and tell him you are here," Jim offered.

The man jumped to his feet and grabbed Jim's arm. "I want to give Bill a little surprise, bless his old heart. I wouldn't want you to spoil the surprise."

Then the man half dragged Jim across the room and stood with him against the wall. The man pulled a blade from his sheath and then glared at Carter. "Now, you be smart, boy. Don't spoil the surprise or your brother will pay the price."

Carter didn't bother to correct the man. He wondered if he should do something to change the book's scene. After all, he wasn't worried about Jim. If Jim was Storm, it might be nice to see him sweat. And if he was just a story character, then he wasn't real anyway.

Carter looked at Jim's face and saw how pale it had gotten. The stranger glared at Carter and pressed the knife harder against Jim's neck so Carter turned back to his task of setting the table without a word. Even if Jim wasn't real, Carter didn't want to see him hurt.

The captain finally stormed into the room, slamming the door behind him. He headed straight toward Carter.

"Bill," the thin stranger called from behind him.

The captain spun and gasped. "Black Dog!"

"We should sit and talk like the old shipmates we are. These boys will fetch us some food and drink, won't you, boys?"

Jim nodded and practically ran from the room. Carter followed him. Almost at once, a fight broke out in the room they had left. They heard furniture knocked over and the clash of swords. Finally, someone cried out in pain.

The boys rushed back to see Black Dog burst out of the inn door. Blood streamed down the man's left arm. The captain ran right behind, still swinging his heavy blade. Black Dog was younger than the captain and soon outran him.

The captain finally turned and headed back for the inn. "Now I can have my breakfast," he gasped.

"Are you hurt?" Jim cried.

"Just get me something to drink," the pirate demanded.

Jim ran for the kitchen. Carter watched the old pirate stagger into the parlor. He nearly made it to the breakfast table. As he reached out a hand toward the chair, he fell. He lay still on the floor, his face a sick shade of grey.

At the crash, Jim and his mother hurried into the room.

"What a disgrace on this house!" Jim's mother cried. She looked over at Jim with worried eyes. "Your poor, sick father."

"What should we do?" Jim asked.

His mother offered no suggestions, but merely twisted her hands together and continued to moan about the disgrace. Then Doctor Livesey walked in.

"Oh, doctor!" Jim cried as he jumped to his feet. "Please help, the captain is wounded."

The doctor bent down and looked at the fallen pirate. "Wounded? No more than you or I. He has had a stroke. Mrs. Hawkins, run up and stay with your husband. I will check on him directly. Do not worry him with this."

Mrs. Hawkins nodded and rushed away, clearly relieved.

"Jim, fetch a basin," he said. "We'll try to save this fellow's worthless life."

Carter watched, swallowing down nausea as the doctor cut into the pirate's arm and let blood run into the basin. He was sure it couldn't be good for a man to lose as much blood as the doctor poured out.

Finally, the pirate opened his eyes. "Where's Black Dog? I'll crush his skull, I will."

"There is no dog here," the doctor said. "You've had a stroke."

The old pirate continued to mutter about skulls as Carter and Jim hauled the man to his feet and half carried him up to his room.

Since Jim's mother was busy with her husband, Jim and Carter tended to the old pirate. Time passed fast, like a dream, though not quite fast enough to make the room spin. Carter realized this must be how the computer was actually designed to close the gaps in the books. You just drift into a new period of time. It was certainly easier on his stomach.

Carter looked around. He was still in the old pirate's room. Jim stood next to the pirate's bed. "Did the doctor say how long I was to lie here?" the pirate asked, his voice thin but excited.

"A week at least," Jim said.

"Ah, they'll get wind of this for sure," the captain muttered. "I'll trick them again. I'm not afraid of them." As he spoke, he pulled himself up, using Jim's shoulder as a crutch. Finally though, the man had to flop back onto the bed. "Oh, Jim, that doctor's done me in for sure."

"Just rest," Jim said.

"I can't get away. They're after my old sea

chest," the captain gasped. "I was first mate on old Flint's crew. I'm the only one who knows the place. I'll need your help if they come back. They'll get the black spot on me for sure."

"The black spot?" Jim asked.

"A summons," the old pirate said. "If they get that on me, I'll need you to take a horse and bring men. All the men you can find. There will be a fight, lad, but we can win the day yet. I'll share with you equals, upon my honor."

The pirate fell asleep then. Carter looked over toward the chest. He wondered if he should grab it now. If Storm was taking Jim's place, then Carter needed to keep the chest away from Jim more than he needed to keep it safe from the pirates of the book.

Before Carter could decide, Jim turned to face him, "Should I tell the doctor?"

"I don't know," Carter said, struggling to remember what Jim did next in the book.

Suddenly a voice called out from beyond the room. Carter recognized it as Jim's mother wailing in sorrow. Carter knew what that meant. Jim's father had died. He looked at the boy and saw the same awareness on his face. Jim raced for the door and Carter followed.

He thought of the look on the other boy's face. Jim must not be Storm. How could the hacker possibly look so sad and shocked over the death of a character in a book? Could Storm really be that good at acting?

THE DEAD MAN'S CHEST

Carter ran out of the room and right into the parlor of the Admiral Benbow Inn. He staggered a moment, since that was impossible—the room was on a different floor of the inn.

"Izzy?" he whispered.

"I'm getting better at these jumps," she said. "I've jumped you ahead over the visit from the blind pirate that kills the captain with shock."

Carter looked into the parlor and saw Jim kneeling beside the captain's body. His mother rushed past Carter and gasped when she saw the body. Jim told his mother about the pirates. He said the captain had warned him that the pirates would return for the chest.

"It must be full of gold," he said.

"The pirates can have it," his mother said. "Though perhaps we could take out what he owes for his room these many days."

"We need to leave," Jim insisted. "The pirates will be coming. We should get help."

"No one will come and help you," Carter warned. "They'll be afraid of the pirates."

"They wouldn't be such cowards," Jim insisted.

"They would," Carter replied.

Jim's mother began crying loudly. "I hate that women are so wimpy in these books," Izzy said in Carter's ear.

"Hush," he snapped.

"Don't speak to my mother that way," Jim said, glaring at him.

"Sorry. Look, you can probably get someone to ride for Dr. Livesey," Carter said, remembering that from the book. "Then we should open the chest before the pirates get here."

"Open the chest!" Jim's mother gasped.

"To get the money owed you," Carter said. "Didn't the captain say you had until ten o'clock? There should be time."

"I'll tell the neighbor," Jim said. "Stay with my mother." He dashed out the door before Carter could answer. Jim didn't leave his mother behind in the book, Carter was sure of it. Did that mean Jim really was Storm or did the story just change because Carter was in it? With both Storm and Izzy making changes, Carter had no idea what might be a clue.

"Perhaps," the woman said shakily, "you could go through the captain's pockets? He may have enough for the room in his pockets. Then we wouldn't need to open the chest."

Carter looked at her. "You want me to touch a dead man?"

"He can't hurt you," she said.

"She's right about that," Izzy offered helpfully in his ear.

"It's still creepy," Carter said, looking down at the sprawled body of the old captain.

"Just do it," Izzy insisted. "You need to get the key to the sea chest."

"Okay," Carter grumbled, kneeling down. The first thing he saw was a slip of paper held in the man's hand. Carter tugged it free.

"What's that?" Jim's mother asked.

"The black spot," Carter said. "It says the pirates are coming at ten tonight." As he spoke those words, a clock chimed six times.

"Six o'clock," the woman said. "We should hurry."

Carter took a deep breath and plunged his hand in the man's coat pockets. He found bits of lint, string, and the man's knife but no money or key. He rocked back on his heels and tried to remember where the key had been in the book. Then he shuddered and slipped his hand between the man's greasy neck and the dirty collar of his shirt and coat. He found a string and pulled. A key dangled.

"You've found it!" Jim's mother said.

Carter cut the string with the pirate's knife

and followed Jim's mother out of the room. At the doorway, he turned a last look to the man on the floor. It didn't seem right to go through his stuff with him laying dead on the floor. He had to remind himself again that this wasn't real.

"Come on, boy," Jim's mother urged, tugging on his arm.

The lock on the sea chest gave easily to the key. As they opened the lid, the scent of tobacco and tar burned Carter's nose. He saw a suit of clothes folded on top.

"Ah, we should bury him in these," Jim's mother said as she set them neatly aside. Under the clothes lay a pair of pistols, a scatter of sea shells, and a bundle wrapped in oil cloth. Carter knew that bundle was the most important thing in the chest. He lifted it out carefully.

A small bag fell from the bundle and landed with a jingle. Jim's mother grabbed it and shook a mix of coins out into her hand.

"I'll take only what we're owed," she said primly. She poked at the coins, frowning.

"What do you suppose these are worth? I've never seen the like."

Carter heard footsteps downstairs. "Just take the whole bag. We need to go," he urged.

"I'll not take more than he owed," she insisted. "I'm an honest woman."

Just then Jim came in, panting from running. "No one would come," he said. "But they promised to get Dr. Livesey."

"That's good," his mother said. "Help me decide what these coins are worth."

"Mother, there's no time. We need to run and hide before the pirates come," he said.

His mother merely returned to muttering over the coins. Carter wondered if he should suggest they pick the woman up and carry her. She was pretty small and kind of skinny. He was pretty sure they could drag her.

Finally she gave in to their urging and they hurried outside. Carter still carried the oilcloth wrapped package with one arm. He helped Jim hustle his mother along with the other. The night was foggy, but he doubted it would offer enough cover.

Between the dark and the sound of the pirates closing in on the inn, it didn't help Carter much to remind himself that this was only a story. After all, Storm had been messing with the program. Carter couldn't begin to guess what surprises he might have thrown in.

"I'm going to faint," Jim's mother whispered and her weight sagged against both boys.

"Fainting," Izzy said, her voice full of disgust. "A real woman wouldn't just flop over like that."

"Not helpful," Carter muttered, then he raised his voice slightly. "There should be an old stone bridge around here. We should hide under that."

He saw Jim's head bob and he nodded off in one direction. They stumbled through the fog, dragging the moaning woman. Finally, they reached the bridge and stuffed her under it.

"You stay with her," Jim said. "I'll go back and check on the pirates."

"Not likely," Carter said. "We'll just let her

rest here while we both go."

Jim frowned but nodded, and both boys headed back toward the inn. They heard the pirates shouting as they searched the inn. Carter spotted the pirate leader, a ragged blind man who leaned heavily on the shoulder of another pirate. The blind man swung his stick sharply at anyone who didn't obey fast enough.

The blind pirate demanded that they find Flint's map, but the others had to admit it wasn't in the open chest.

"Those boys have it!" the blind pirate shouted. "Spread out and find them."

"What map?" Jim asked.

"This one," Carter said, hefting the wrapped package. "If they find it, they'll kill us for sure."

Suddenly, they heard horses and pistol shots. The pirates scattered, leaving the old blind leader to rant and call after them. He stumbled around swinging his stick. Riders galloped over the rise of the hill.

The hoofbeats must have panicked the blind

pirate. Still yelling, he ran right under one of the horses. The rider couldn't stop in time and the horse ran the blind man down.

The riders were soldiers sent by the neighbor Jim had talked to. The man had run for Dr. Livesey's house but met with the soldiers on the road and sent them instead. The soldiers helped bring Jim's mother back to the inn. She moaned when she saw how the pirates had wrecked the inn during their search.

"What could they have been after?" one of the officers asked.

"This," Carter said, hefting the package. "We need to take this to Dr. Livesey at once. It's adventure time."

The soldier looked at him in confusion. He finally agreed to take the boys to Livesey since he needed to go there and report anyway.

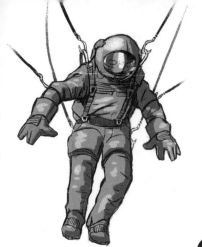

THE
JOURNEY
BEGINS

Carter followed the officer out the inn door and straight into a large, well-lit room. He stumbled in surprise, then realized Izzy was jumping them across time in the book again.

"You could warn a guy," he muttered.

"Where would be the fun in that?" she asked.

"We're not here for fun," Carter reminded her. She didn't answer and he knew they were both thinking about Uncle Dan.

"Carter," Jim called, "come and look at this map. You found it, you should see it."

Carter walked over and looked down at the paper the doctor has spread carefully out on a table. He saw an island shaped a bit like a fat dragon. He remembered that was right according to the book. Three hills were drawn on the map. "The Spyglass" was scrawled across one of the hills. Three crosses were marked at other spots. He remembered that from the book as well.

But now a skull with bones crossed below it settled at the end of an inlet. It looked like a pirate symbol, but the skull was far oversized and almost seemed part of the island. At another place, a dark blot nearly pierced the map paper as if drawn furiously. The blot was labeled, "Death and deep."

Carter swallowed. Were these additions from Izzy or Storm? He quickly turned the paper over as he remembered there were more directions on the back. They seemed to be the same as Carter remembered. There were directions for taking a bearing from a tree on Spyglass, and more about hills and crags. Then he saw a last reference: "Within the skull, bright fires that burn. Yo, ho, ho." That definitely wasn't in the book, but as clues go, it didn't tell Carter much.

"Tomorrow I start for Bristol," the squire said. Carter looked up at him. Though Carter was tall, the squire was still taller and broad shouldered. His face was sun dark and wrinkled around the eyes. "We'll sail for the treasure in three weeks."

"I'm going on this hunt, as is Jim," the doctor said. "Will you join us, Carter?"

"I will," Carter said.

"Okay, look close at those three," Izzy said. "Storm has to be one of them. They're the ones who are in the book from the time of finding the map to the end. Do any of them look suspicious?"

Carter watched the three quietly. The squire and the doctor talked about preparations for the trip and they sounded pretty much like Carter remembered. The doctor even scolded the squire about not keeping secrets well. Jim mostly listened. Carter looked at Jim closest of all. Jim was in every moment of the book, so he'd be the best person of all to take over. But even though Carter stared, he saw nothing unusual in the other boy's face.

"I'm going to do a big jump now," Izzy warned. "I'm afraid this one is going to spin."

"Terrific," Carter muttered as he waited for the room and people around him to spin. That's when a thought hit him. *The real book characters wouldn't feel the spin, but Storm would. Storm was a person just like him and should feel the same disorientation when they jumped.*

Carter locked eyes on Jim just as the room spun. The blur hit so suddenly that he couldn't tell if Jim looked surprised, but he'd look again as soon as the spinning stopped.

Carter could smell salty air and old fish. The floor under his feet continued to dip and sway even after the spinning had stopped. He looked around sharply for Jim and found him looking up at an old sailor with earrings in his ears and squinty eyes. The squire stood beside them, grinning as if he'd already found the treasure.

Neither looked dizzy.

"Either Jim isn't Storm," Carter whispered for Izzy's sake, "or he adapts to your spinning jumps a lot better than I do. And the way the squire is smiling, he can't be feeling as sick as I do."

"Can you see the doctor?" Izzy asked.

Carter spotted the doctor standing near the rail, looking toward a sharp-looking man who seemed angry with everything and everyone. "He has a hand on the rail," Carter said. "Maybe he needed it to steady himself. He could be Storm."

"Keep an eye on him," Izzy suggested.

"You think?" Carter replied, his voice thick with sarcasm.

"Come on, Carter," Jim called out. "We're heading to the cabin."

Carter followed Jim and the squire. The doctor caught up and walked at his side. They had barely walked into the cabin when a sailor rapped on the door frame.

"Captain Smollett, sir, is asking to speak with you," he said.

"I am always at the captain's orders," the squire said cheerfully. "Show him in."

The captain had clearly been close behind the sailor. He strode in quickly and shut the door behind him.

"Well, Captain," the squire boomed, "is all shipshape and seaworthy?"

"I shall speak plain," the captain said. "I don't like this treasure hunt. I don't like the crew, nor my first officer."

The squire puffed up and began ranting, but the doctor cut in quickly. "Could you tell us your specific complaints?"

"Every man aboard seems to know more about this trip than I," the captain said. "I did not know this was a treasure hunt when I signed on. Treasure is ticklish work. And I would have liked to choose my own crew."

"Do you have specific complaints of the men?" the doctor asked.

"The first officer is too free with the crew," he said. "He doesn't keep the distance he needs to be a good officer."

"What can we do?" the doctor asked. He put a hand on the squire's arm, since the man looked about ready to explode.

"Move weapons to the hold under this cabin to keep them out of harm's way. And keep all the people you trust close to you and your cabin."

"Those seem like reasonable precautions," the doctor said. "We can do that."

"You are a smart man, doctor," the captain said. "When I came down here, I intended to quit this voyage, but I see you are a man who listens to reason." He turned a pointed look toward the squire.

"I will do as you desire," the squire snapped. "But I think the worse of you."

The captain nodded. "As you please. You'll find I do my duty." Then he left as briskly as he had come.

"Squire," the doctor said, "I believe you have brought two fine and honest men on this voyage, the captain and Long John Silver."

"I like Silver well enough," the squire said.

Again time passed in a dreamlike way. Carter was vaguely aware of the moving of weapons and the new berths for the most trusted men. Carter, Jim, and the doctor's groundskeeper were assigned to one cabin.

Carter heard Long John Silver complaining about all the changes. "We'll miss the morning tide!"

"My order," the captain told him. "I believe you'll be needed below. The crew will want supper."

Carter jumped at that. He'd forgotten the old pirate had signed on as cook at first. Then the captain called out for Jim and Carter to head down and help the cook. They were greeted by Silver's parrot shouting, "Pieces of eight! Pieces of eight!"

Long John Silver gave them some chores, and

again Carter had the vague feeling of working hard. But time passed too fast to be normal. Finally, the scene sharpened and Carter found himself alone with Jim.

"I'm hungry," Jim said. "I'm going to get an apple from the barrel on deck."

Carter perked up, remembering the apple barrel. "I'll come with."

Jim shrugged and they headed up to find the deck quiet. The only sounds were the swish of the sea against the side of the ship and the soft whistling of the man at the ship's wheel.

Jim peered over the side of a huge barrel. "I can't see the bottom in the dark," he complained. "Give me a boost so I can climb in."

Carter made his hands into stirrups and Jim scrambled into the barrel with a soft thump. Since he was considerably taller, Carter was able to jump and boost himself in after Jim.

"I didn't know you were joining me, cousin," Jim said when Carter just missed landing on his head. "I've bad news. The barrel is empty."

"It would be a great hideout," Carter said.

Jim sat back against the side and considered it. "Feels like sitting in a well and too snug with both of us."

Suddenly, Carter heard the thumping of Long John Silver's peg leg and crutch. He shushed Jim softly. The barrel trembled when someone leaned his shoulder against it.

"I lost my leg when I was quartermaster aboard Flint's ship," Silver said.

"Flint was the flower of the flock," another voice called out.

"Even so, his men were all begging before they came aboard here," Silver said. "They made poor use of their fortune. I can see you're different. You're young and smart as paint."

Jim gasped softly and Carter put his hand over the other boy's mouth. He knew Silver had flattered Jim with the exact same words in another part of the book. It was one of the spots Izzy had skipped over.

"We'll live easy after this voyage," Silver said.

"But we won't be able to show our faces," the younger man said.

"You'll need to be careful," Silver said. "That's true. But treasure can ease a lot of cares."

"I'm with you," the other man said.

"Brave and smart," Silver said, shaking the other man's hand so heartily that the barrel trembled. "I knew it when I clapped my eyes on you."

By the sound of the footsteps, the younger man hurried away. Silver gave a whistle and soon another came and sat.

"He's square," Silver said.

"I knew he would be. He's no fool." Carter searched his memory for which character this would be. This must be Israel Hand. Carter swallowed hard, remembering what a vicious pirate the man was.

"I've had about enough of the captain working us half to death," the pirate grumbled. "And I'm not the only one."

"We're letting the captain find the island for

us," Silver said. "Not one of us can navigate as well as he. We'll settle with him soon enough."

"We'll hold off," Hand said. "But we'll want our bit of fun soon."

"Soon enough," Silver said. "When we're on the island, the captain and his friends will have their end. I'll wring the squire's neck myself."

Jim trembled beside Carter in the barrel. Then the light in the barrel brightened and Carter could see Jim's wide eyes. The moon had risen and shown into the barrel. At almost the same time, a voice shouted, "Land ho!"

TREASURE ISLAND

The pirates near the barrel joined the great rush to the deck rail to search for land. Carter boosted Jim out of the barrel and then followed him. Both boys looked around. Carter spotted Dr. Livesey at the rail.

"Has anyone aboard seen this Skull Island before?" the captain called above the babble.

"I have," Silver called. "That great hill at the center is called Spyglass. I've seen it used for a lookout while ships lay at anchor to the south."

"Show me on this chart," the captain said.

Silver nearly ran to look at the map the captain held, but his disappointment was clear when he grew close. The map was a copy of the old pirate's map without any of the clues and notes. Silver covered his disappointment quickly and gave directions for safely bringing the ship to anchor.

After the captain dismissed him, Silver stumped over to Jim and Carter. "Skeleton Island is a sweet spot," he told them. "You must come ashore. You can swim, climb trees, and hunt goats. It's a great island to explore. I'll make you both a snack to bring along."

Silver clapped Jim on the back and hobbled off.

Doctor Livesey called to Jim then. Carter saw Jim whispering to the doctor, and he knew Jim was telling the doctor what he'd overheard. Carter watched the doctor's face, but the man gave nothing away. Still, he was more and more sure that Dr. Livesey must be Storm.

The doctor stepped over to speak to the captain and the squire. Then the captain called for all hands on deck and announced that everyone was going to get a small break and a cup of grog to celebrate the safe arrival at the island.

The crew cheered at that news. Then the captain, the squire, and the doctor went below to their cabin. Not long after, word came that Jim Hawkins and Carter Lewis were wanted in the cabin.

Jim launched into his story as soon as the boys got to the cabin. Carter watched the three men closely as Jim spoke. Not one of them moved. They all kept their eyes on Jim's face from his first word. Finally, he was done.

"Captain," said the squire, "it seems you were right and I was wrong."

"I saw no signs of mutiny," the captain said. "I have never seen a crew hide its plans so well."

"I believe Silver is the cause of that," the doctor said. "He's a remarkable man."

The talk then moved on to whom they could trust and who was certainly on Silver's side. They decided the good guys numbered eight, counting Carter. A plan was made to split up Silver's men and leave fewer to fight aboard ship.

The captain recommended that all the men they trusted be armed at once. Carter noticed they didn't offer guns to him or Jim, but he was okay with that. He figured he'd only end up shooting himself in the leg.

The weather had turned hot and the crew grumbled aloud for the first time. The captain pretended not to hear it. Silver pointed off toward the woods and told the captain a stockade stood beyond where they could see.

"It looks swampy. There's fever here too," the doctor said, frowning. "I am sure of it."

When the captain announced shore leave, the crew cheered again. The captain asked Silver to arrange the parties and equip them with snacks if they needed them. Then the captain hurried back to his cabin.

It was clear that every man wanted to go ashore, but Silver put a quick stop to that. In the end, six stayed aboard and thirteen took to the long boats, including Silver.

Jim poked Carter. "Let's go ashore."

Normally Carter would have called him crazy, but he was sure Izzy must be planning another clue. He blinked as he realized that the doctor wouldn't be coming ashore. He wouldn't see Izzy's clue. Did that mean, he wasn't Storm?

Carter looked sharply at Jim again, suddenly sure the boy must be Storm. "Sure, maybe we can help."

Jim and Carter jumped into the boats just as they launched. No one moved to stop them, though Carter saw Silver eye them sharply. The boat the boys were in reached shore first and they both swung themselves out using low-hanging branches. They hit the ground running.

"Jim! Carter!" Long John Silver called after them, but the boys never stopped running.

At first the ground was swampy, but finally they reached open, sandy land. They saw only a few trees, all twisted by wind. Ahead, Carter made out a hill with two peaks.

"It's good to be off the ship," Jim said quietly.

Carter nodded. They walked for a while,

until Jim pointed to the brush to one side of them. Carter heard a sound like a slow leak from a bicycle tire.

"Snake," Jim said. "And we're probably the first people it's ever seen."

"Snake?" Carter said in alarm. That hissing was far closer and louder than he cared for. He liked his snakes in zoos and pet shops, not on the ground near his leg.

Jim led the climb up the hill. When they reached the top, they could see the outline of Spyglass through the haze that came off the steaming swampy areas.

"Wouldn't it be great if we found the treasure?" Jim asked, his voice excited.

Before he could answer, the boys were startled by a flock of birds taking to the air all at once. "Someone's coming," Jim said.

Carter suddenly remembered that someone died in this scene. He didn't want it to be him. He turned with Jim to look for someplace to hide. Quickly, the boys crawled into thick brush near the base of a tree.

They could hear voices close by. Carter recognized one as Silver. The men stopped just out of sight.

"We need to get closer," Jim whispered.

Carter wasn't really sure he wanted to be any closer, but when Jim crawled toward the sounds, he followed. The boys kept low in the rough scrub. Finally, they could make out the words.

"I'm only talking to you because I think so highly of you, Tom," Silver said.

"What is a man like you doing with this mess of swabs?" Tom asked. "You've money of your own and an honest name. You're too brave to have thrown in with them from fear. What made you turn against duty?"

Suddenly, they heard shouts in the distance, followed by a long scream. "What was that?" Tom gasped.

"I imagine that was Alan," Silver said.

"God rest his soul," Tom said. "I may die like

a dog, but I'll die an honest man like poor Alan. Kill me if you can." Then he turned and set off toward the beach. He didn't go far. Silver flung his crutch at him, knocking him down. Then Silver hopped toward him, using low-hanging branches to help his speed. He stabbed the man in the back. Carter heard low grunts but wasn't sure if they came from the dying man or Silver.

"It's not real. It's not real," Carter whispered, fighting the urge to throw up at the violence.

Silver stood, wiped off his knife, and picked up his crutch. He pulled out a whistle and whistled for his men. Jim was already crawling back away from the scene, and Carter followed. They crawled until they were well clear, then they ran until they couldn't breathe. Finally, they collapsed in a heap, certain they'd outrun the pirates. For several minutes, they simply lay on the ground and panted.

"What's that?" Jim gasped.

Carter looked up to see a shaggy figure leap behind a tree. He staggered to his feet and called out, "Come on out. Don't be afraid. We won't hurt you."

"What are you talking about?" Jim said.

A dark, shaggy man stepped out from hiding and threw himself on his knees. "I'm poor Ben Gunn, and I haven't seen a soul in three years."

Ben Gunn wore clothes made of patches held together by buttons, sticks, and black string. His hair and beard were long and thickly matted.

"Were you shipwrecked?" Jim asked.

The man shook his head. "Marooned," he replied. "I've lived on goats and berries and oysters for these three years. You wouldn't happen to have a piece of cheese?"

"If we can get aboard again, I'll bring you the biggest brick of cheese I can find," Jim promised.

"You haven't come from Flint's ship?" the man asked, fear thick in his voice.

"Flint is dead," Jim said. "But there are some of Flint's hands aboard, including Silver."

Ben Gunn moaned. "If you were sent by Long John Silver, I'm as dead as pork."

Jim told the man the whole story of their adventure.

The man nodded. "If I were to throw in with you and your squire, do you think I might find passage home. And perhaps a bit of the treasure?"

"I'm sure everyone would agree," Jim said. "We'll need all the hands we can get to get rid of the pirates."

Ben then told the boys how he'd once been part of Flint's crew. That's how he knew about the island. Then he'd come back to the island on a treasure hunt of his own.

"I tried to find the treasure," Ben said. "But we looked and looked and never looked it in the eye. And so the men left me here alone to die. But Ben is smarter than they thought."

He ended by saying he had a small boat of his own that the boys could use to get back aboard ship without the pirates seeing him.

Suddenly the sound of a cannon broke the quiet of the island. "The fight has begun," Jim said.

The three ran back toward shore, with Ben shouting out directions now and then to keep them on course. Finally, they skidded to a stop when they spotted the sight of a British flag fluttering in the wind above the tops of the trees.

"I can go no farther," Ben said, "until you come back telling me it's safe. You go. Find your squire. Come back for me when you can."

Strike One

Carter and Jim crouched in the brush beyond the stockade while cannon shots roared from the ship.

"Do you think the pirates have taken over the stockade?" Jim asked.

"No, they would be flying a pirate flag if they had," Carter answered.

As soon as the cannon fire stopped, the boys crept to the stockade wall and scrambled over. After a warm welcome, each side told their story of what the other had missed.

"We lost Redruth," the squire said, looking sadly toward a shadowy corner where the man's body lay covered.

"You did what you could," the captain said, giving the squire a kind pat on the back. "I've never seen a finer shot than you."

"We also lost most of our provisions," the

doctor added.

"And now," the captain said, "we have plenty of work to do." He gave each person a job. Jim and Carter were set to watch the door.

Eventually the doctor walked up to the door. "Do you believe Ben Gunn is trustworthy?" he asked.

"I'm not even sure he's sane," Jim said.

"I believe he meant every word he said," Carter added. "He's desperate to get off this island."

"And get some cheese," Jim added with a grin.

"I have a bit of Parmesan cheese here in this tin. I'll give it to Ben Gunn and see what good he can do us."

"Do you think we have a chance?" Jim asked.

"The pirates are camping in the swamp where fever is sure to find them quickly," the doctor said. "And they have no discipline and little loyalty. I'm not ready to give up on us yet."

The boys' turn as guards passed and they

settled down to sleep. It seemed Carter had barely laid down before someone was shouting. Silver was coming to the stockade under a flag of truce.

"Carter?" Izzy said.

"Yeah," he whispered.

"The last clue is coming up here," she said. "So you need to figure out who Storm is before Storm finds the treasure from the clues."

Carter sat blinking. He wasn't sure he'd seen all the clues. He thought a moment. The map had changed. There was a dark blot where none had been. And there was a skull on the map. He was sure the book didn't have any skulls, but he'd heard about skulls several times.

And hadn't Ben Gunn said something about an eye? Could that have been a clue? Skulls have eye holes. Maybe there was a skull somewhere on the island that held the new directions to the treasure? Did that mean the blot wasn't a clue?

Carter finally shook off his rambling thoughts and watched Silver struggling up the hill toward

Captain Smollett. Carter couldn't make out what they said. He walked closer to stand beside Jim as Silver flopped in the sand.

Carter watched as Long John Silver tried a combination of charm and threats to get the map away from the captain. The captain merely stood ramrod straight and refused to consider anything except total surrender from the pirates.

Finally, the captain told Silver to leave.

"Give me a hand up!" the pirate cried.

"Not I," returned the captain.

"Who'll give me a hand up?" Silver looked at all of them, but no one stepped forward. Finally, the pirate had to crawl through the sand until he reached the porch to haul himself to his feet.

"We'll be on you before the hour!" Silver yelled.

"If you're a smart man, you'll run and hide," Captain Smollett replied. "Hide in the hills or under them. Hide on the ship or in a cave. But hide or something bad will be on you."

Carter stared at the captain. That speech definitely wasn't in the book. It must be the clue Izzy mentioned. But the captain hadn't said anything about a skull. He had said "hide" over and over. Maybe combined with the earlier skull clues, Izzy was telling them something was hidden in a skull. But what skull and where?

Carter looked around at the others to see if the captain's speech had any affect. If it did, he saw no sign. Storm was too good at acting, he guessed.

The captain stormed back to the stockade as Silver scrambled back over the far stockade wall. He scolded everyone for being away from their posts, then gave orders to prepare for the coming attack.

The hour passed quickly and Silver's men attacked. At first, bullets struck the log house. The men inside fired more than a few in return. Jim and Carter dashed from man to man, reloading weapons after each firing. Jim was definitely faster at reloading. Carter heard more than one grumbling complaint or hissed command to hurry.

Finally, the pirates swarmed over the stockade wall and rushed the log house. The house had grown so smoky from gunshot that everyone was half smothered and no one could see.

"Out lads!" the captain shouted. "Fight them in the open!"

Carter grabbed a cutlass at the same moment as Jim, and saw his blade slice across Jim's knuckles. He didn't pause to apologize but turned and rushed outside. Carter ran into a pirate and began flailing away with his cutlass. He didn't know if it was luck or the program, but he managed to smack the pirate's right arm with the flat of his blade and send the pirate's weapon flying.

The man went after his blade and Carter chased him halfway down the hill. More pirates were running and Carter whooped with the thrill. Then he heard the doctor shouting,

"Back to cover! Fire from the house!"

Carter reluctantly turned and ran for the log house. As he ran, he looked at fallen pirates and then the wounded and dead in the log house. He knew they weren't real, but he felt sad anyway. Somehow when he thought about adventures, he never pictured people actually dying.

This thought led him to worry again about Uncle Dan. He had to figure out which of these people was Storm and put an end to this. Uncle Dan needed him. Carter joined in to help with making supper as he considered each of his suspects.

Then after they ate, he spotted Dr. Livesey pick up the map of the island and a gun. Carter remembered that the doctor went off alone at this point to find Ben Gunn. He realized that if Storm was the doctor, this would be a perfect time to go and collect the treasure and end the contest.

He looked between Dr. Livesey and Jim. If he let the doctor leave alone and he was Storm, his uncle would pay the price for his mistake. Carter knew that not long after the doctor left, Jim would leave as well to find Ben Gunn's boat and reclaim the ship from the pirates. If Carter followed the doctor and was wrong, it would be the perfect chance for Jim to solve the clues and win.

He had to make his choice now and make it right. Jim was in every moment of the book, he would be the best choice if Storm wanted to take over a character. But the doctor was in nearly as many scenes and was an adult. Somehow Carter didn't think Storm would pick the kid. He was too scornful of children.

Crossing his fingers and hoping he was right, Carter slipped away from the fire and followed Dr. Livesey toward the north stockade fence. The doctor never turned around, but Carter slunk along, keeping his distance so the doctor wouldn't hear him.

The coolness of the tree line was a welcome relief from the smoky heat of the stockade. The doctor's stride was long and Carter had to hurry to keep up. He realized he was incredibly tired and wondered how many hours he'd been in the suit without anything to eat. Just thinking about it made his stomach growl.

Carter quickly noticed that the doctor didn't seem to be looking around. He never called out to Ben either. Carter felt a rush of excitement. It looked like he could be right. If the doctor was not out here looking for Ben, then he must be Storm.

In that case, all he had to do was stand up and call him out. He closed the gap between them in a few trotting strides and called out, "Storm!"

The doctor turned around and looked at Carter in surprise and confusion. "It's a clear night. I see no sign of a storm. What are you doing out here, Carter? The captain needs you back at the stockade."

"Don't pretend," Carter said. "I know you're Storm and you're here looking for the treasure."

"Storm?" the doctor looked more confused. "I don't know what you're talking about. Are you feverish?" The doctor stepped closer and placed a hand on Carter's forehead, before he could back away. "You feel cool enough."

"Izzy?" Carter said. "Doesn't Storm have to admit to it once I find him?"

"I don't think that's Storm," Izzy said quietly.

"Oh no," Carter muttered.

"What are you babbling about, boy?" the doctor said. "Let's find you a place to sit. I'll help you back to the others as soon as I find Ben Gunn. I'm sure he's lurking around the pirate camp. I should be able to circle around and approach them from this ground just over there." He pointed off into the darkness. "But do be quiet now."

Carter groaned. The doctor was on his book mission after all. Carter had made the wrong first guess. Storm must be Jim.

"I have to get back to the stockade," Carter said.

94

"I don't think you should wander around in the dark," the doctor said. "Wait here. I'll be back." He hurried ahead, turning to look worriedly back at Carter several times.

"Can I just call out Jim now? Choose him from here?" Carter asked.

"Are you sure it's him?" Izzy asked. "Are you totally positive? You don't have room to make a mistake. You only have one guess left."

Carter was sure. Well, he was mostly sure. Suddenly, he wasn't sure at all. "I'm going to go find Ben Gunn's boat. If I can find it, I should be able to see if Jim is on his book mission or trying to solve the treasure hunt."

"Hurry," Izzy said.

Carter hurried.

FINDING STORM

Carter knew Ben Gunn's boat was hidden on the shore near a white rock. So first, Carter headed for the shore. Since everything on the island rose uphill away from the shore, all he had to do was head downhill and he would hit the shoreline sooner or later.

At first, he stuck to the clear trail that he and the doctor had followed. He couldn't follow it all the way down since he didn't want to run into the stockade. He began angling through the brush away from the stockade and toward where he guessed the boat was anchored.

Suddenly, he heard voices and laughing. He'd nearly stumbled into the pirate camp. He froze and carefully backed up a bit until the sounds were muted, then he began circling the camp.

The ground was damp and slightly mushy. He remembered from the book that the pirates were getting sick with some kind of swamp fever.

"I can't get sick from the fever in the book, can I?" he whispered.

"Of course not," Izzy said. "I'm sure Uncle Dan's suits don't blow viruses up your nose."

"I didn't think so," Carter muttered.

"You can get sick from not eating though," Izzy said. "So the sooner we win this, the better you're going to feel."

"Sick, how?" Carter asked.

"Dizzy, headaches," Isabelle said. "Just hurry and don't worry about it."

"Sure," Carter answered, then immediately noticed his head did hurt a little.

"Focus," Izzy said.

Carter didn't answer as he slunk through the trees around the pirate camp. Finally, he walked out of the tree line and onto the beach. He looked back and could now make out the faint glimmer of the pirate fire through the trees. Night was beginning to fall and a thick fog made it seem later than it was.

Carter looked out across the water. The fog blurred details and he couldn't tell sea from sky. Still he made out lights and knew they must come from the ship anchored out there.

Carter turned and followed the shore, scanning always for the large white rock that was supposed to mark the position of Ben Gunn's boat. With the fog on the beach, he stumbled and fell more than once. Finally, the white rock loomed out of the grey ahead of him and he heard the sound of something dragging on the sand.

Carter crept quietly around the rock. He saw Jim hauling a small boat up onto his shoulder so he could drag it toward the shore. Carter knew that in the book Jim would paddle out to the larger ship and cut it free to drift away from the shore and the pirates. Did the sight of Jim with the boat mean he was holding true to his story role? If so, did that mean Jim wasn't Storm either?

He crept after Jim, sometimes crawling in the sand to keep from being spotted. Jim hauled the boat toward the water, stumbling often. Finally, Jim splashed out to waist deep water, pushing the small boat ahead of him. Then he hoisted himself over the side.

Carter watched, unsure of what to do next. Should he let Jim know he was there and join him so he could watch for clues that Jim was Storm? What if he wasn't Storm? Couldn't the hacker be setting off to hunt the treasure right now?

"Jim!" Carter called.

"Carter?" the boy's voice was thick with surprise. "Is the doctor back?"

"I don't think so," Carter said. "What are you doing?"

"I'm going to cut the ship free."

"I'll come with you."

"Can you not see this boat?" Jim asked. "We

won't both fit."

"Okay," Carter said. "I'll wait for you at the stockade."

"Take care, cousin."

"You too."

Carter backed away, still unsure of whether he should have stuck with Jim. He slunk back toward the pirate camp. He knew the pirates had the boats from the ship. He knew also that the pirates weren't great at keeping watch. If he waited for them to fall asleep, maybe he could steal one of the boats and head out to keep an eye on Jim.

He huddled in the dark near the camp until the sounds all died down to snores. Then he snuck over to the boat that lay close by on the sand. It was a much longer, heavier boat than the one Jim had taken. It was all Carter could do to drag it into the water. He was grateful for the pirates' natural laziness. They hadn't bothered to haul it far up on shore.

Once in the water, he found the boat wasn't

easy to handle. It was clearly designed for more than one man. Carter remembered his boating lessons from the summer he'd gone to camp and rowed like crazy. He peered out across the water. He couldn't see the big ship anywhere. Jim must already have cut it loose and be riding the current.

Carter poured the last of his strength into rowing the boat out into the current. Then he could simply let it go to follow the same path Jim was sending the big ship on. He hoped he was making the right choice. He had a strong sense that his time was running out.

Carter knew the boat was drifting north and that he needed to watch for an inlet into the trees where the larger ship would have ended up. Tired as he was, he used the oars now and then to speed him on. Finally, he spotted the place and began rowing with fresh energy. As he closed in on it, he saw the great ship run aground and tilt steeply to one side.

Carter turned the small ship off to the sand

as well and scrambled out. He ran across the sand in time to see Jim wading to shore. He'd made it just in time. "Jim!"

"Cousin!" the surprise on Jim's face nearly made Carter laugh, until he saw Jim's bloodied sleeve.

"You're bleeding."

"In more than one place," Jim said, grinning. "But I'm alive and we've got the *Hispaniola* back from the pirates."

"Good job." Carter grinned, then suddenly he nearly stumbled. The little inlet where the ship was run aground was much lower on one side of the water than on the other. As Carter looked past Jim's head, he saw a rock rising up across the water.

The dawning sun on the steep rocks gave one of the huge boulders the rounded shine of a skull. It had two matching openings, one shallow and the other deep like a cave. The openings looked like the eyes of a skull. Below this skull outcropping, two trees had fallen.

Their trunks crossed as they leaned against the rocks like crossed bones.

Carter jerked his eyes away before Jim could realize what he'd seen. That was the skull from the map, but the real *Treasure Island* had no such skull. This was Izzy's addition and the solution to her challenge. Carter was sure the treasure lay in the deep eyehole of the skull.

"Where to now?" Carter asked.

"We need to get back and let the others know about the ship," Jim said.

Carter nodded silently.

"Good plan, but I think I'll stay here with the ship," Carter said. "I'll defend it if the pirates find it."

Jim nodded. "Sounds smart. Good luck to you." Then he turned and headed off into the woods. Carter watched him go. Surely that meant Jim wasn't Storm either. He knew the hacker would be suspicious of Carter wanting to avoid all the action.

Still, if Carter just sat in the eye of the skull,

all he had to do was wait for someone to come along. Whoever showed up would have to be Storm.

Carter turned and began wading into the water. It would require a bit of a swim to reach the other side, but he should manage it easily enough, even as tired as he was. At least the water was warm.

Suddenly a spray of water kicked up beside Carter's leg. Someone was shooting at him! Carter yelped and spun. He saw a shadowy figure in the wood line and the unmistakable line of a gun.

"Don't shoot!" he yelled.

"But I need you out of the way," a high, thin voice called out. Carter didn't recognize it, but he suspected it was someone changing his voice to fool him. He squinted at the shadow but couldn't make out any details. It seemed too tall to be Jim, and that's about all he could guess.

"Storm?" he said.

"It's not enough to find me," the high voice

said. "You must guess which character I play. And you only have one guess left."

"Because you're not Dr. Livesey," Carter said.

"Correct."

"But you have to reach the treasure," Carter said. "And as soon as I see you go for it, I'll know who you are."

"Not if I shoot you right now," the figure answered.

Carter swallowed hard. He was pretty sure Uncle Dan's virtual reality suit wouldn't actually kill him, but it could hurt him. And if he was shot in the head, it might kick him out of the program. He wouldn't have a chance to guess which character was Storm. Shaking, he realized he needed to guess. He needed to do it right now, and he needed to be right.

Storm wasn't Dr. Livesey or Jim. That meant he wasn't a character from the early parts of the book. It had to be someone who came in later. Captain Smollett? Long John Silver? He was pretty sure the legendary pirate would appeal to Storm.

Carter felt his stomach clench hard when he heard the sound of the gun's hammer pulled back. "It's nothing personal," the high voice said. "Nothing much. Now stand still. It will hurt less if I get a clean shot. I'm the best shot on the island, but this gun is pretty old."

The best shot on the island. Suddenly, Carter knew who to guess.

THE BLOWING STORM

"**Y**ou're Squire Trelawney," Carter shouted. "The best shot on the island!"

As soon as he'd shouted the words, the whole world turned pitch black. Carter screamed, certain that Storm had gone through with his threat and shot him. His scream sounded doubly loud in the close confines of the suit. He flailed around, desperate to get free.

He felt Izzy pulling at the back of the suit. He scrambled out so fast, he tripped while pulling out his leg and ended up tumbling onto the floor.

"He shot me," he gasped.

Izzy shook her head. "No, he didn't. The program shut down because you guessed right.

Storm was Squire Trelawney."

"Really?" Carter looked up at her in amazement. He'd guessed right. "He played the part perfectly. I never suspected him until that very last crack about being the best shot on the island. He almost won."

"Now, the question is," Izzy said, "will he be true to his word and let Uncle Dan go."

Carter scrambled to his feet just as the phone in her hand buzzed. She put it on speakerphone instantly.

"Good guess," the robot voice intoned. "But it was close."

"Are you going to let Uncle Dan go?" Izzy said.

"You won this battle," the voice answered. "But I will find a way to win the war."

"That doesn't answer my question," Izzy said. "Are you going to let Uncle Dan go? Are you going to keep your word?"

"Your uncle is a free man," Storm said. "But I'm not done. You never know when a storm will blow in."

The call ended. Isabelle stared at the phone in her hand. "Do you think he's telling the truth? Will he let Uncle Dan go?"

"I hope so," Carter said. "And I don't mean to ruin this moment and all, but I really have to go to the bathroom."

Izzy rolled her eyes at him but didn't say anything. She just stepped aside as Carter dashed past her.

In a little while, they sat together on the stools in Uncle Dan's kitchen. Izzy was staring at her cell phone that lay on the counter in front of her. Carter ate more pickles and grumbled about the lack of food.

"Next time, pack a lunch," she snapped. Then she looked over at her cousin. "Do you think we should call the police? If Storm let him go, he should have called by now."

They both jumped when they heard a ringtone. Izzy snatched at her phone, then they both realized the sound was coming from

Carter's pocket. Shrugging in apology, he pulled out his phone.

"I don't recognize the number," he said. He pushed the button and put the phone to his ear.

"Carter," Uncle Dan's voice was clear in his ear, "I'm on a landline. I don't want to talk long. It's not secure."

Carter whooped and pushed the speakerphone button. "Uncle Dan, are you okay?"

"Sure," their uncle said. "I'm fine. I lost my cell phone somewhere. I just wanted to let you guys know that the hacker got away. So be careful. I'm coming home."

"But what about the kidnapping?" Izzy shouted.

"Kidnapping?" Uncle Dan said. "I don't know what you're talking about, Izzy. I haven't had time to watch the news. You guys can catch me up when I get home. Look, I've been on an open line long enough. See you soon."

They both heard the click of the dial tone and

looked at one another with wide eyes. Uncle Dan hadn't been kidnapped. It was all some kind of trick. What if they'd lost the challenge? What if they'd trashed Uncle Dan's stuff?

Carter put his hand to his stomach as the pickles threatened to rebel. "He fooled us."

Izzy nodded, but then she smiled. "Maybe so," she said. "But he didn't beat us. That's what counts. He didn't beat us."

Carter nodded, but he shuddered when he wondered if they would be so lucky next time.

Carter and Isabelle beat Storm to save their uncle . . . only to find out Uncle Dan was safe all along. They are more determined than ever to find the hacker and put him (or her) behind bars!

Follow the adventure in

Book 4
Lightning Strikes Twice
Escaping Great Expectations